Children's Morals & Manners

Four Volumes of Modern Day Short Stories Teaching the Values of Good Morals and Proper Manners

Volume I

Dude, Lying Isn't Cool

8 Short Stories of Those Who Found Out Why

Published in the United States of America

Triune Group, Inc. – Publishing Division

Library of Congress number pending

2nd Edit 11-4-19

Richard L. McBain

ISBN-10: 1523304367

ISBN-13: 978-1523304363

DEDICATION

This book series is dedicated to my Grandchildren

Nathan, Cade, Mattie, and Carter McBain

BOOK PROVERB

(that gives advice about how people should live)

The importance of being truthful,
Is a most wonderful thing you see,
For it is the real substance,
That gives you integrity!

Integrity - the quality of being honest and having strong moral principles; moral uprightness. "he is known to be a man (or woman) of integrity"

CONTENTS

ACKNOWLEDGEMENTS

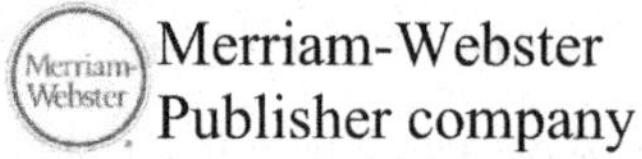

Merriam-Webster, Inc., which was originally the G & C Merriam Company of Springfield, Massachusetts, is an American company that publishes reference books, especially dictionaries that are descendants ... Wikipedia

DOLLAR PHOTO CLUB
www.dollarphotoclub.com

CHAPTER ONE
ACCIDENTS HAPPEN

Whack went the bat when Bobby hit the ball hard and started to run to first base. Tommy went running back after the ball that just happened to crash through Mrs. Jones window.

Everybody began to run in all directions to get out of sight before Mrs. Jones would come out to see who was responsible for breaking her window.
Tommy was still standing near her window when Mrs. Jones came out with the ball. "Did you break my window?" asked an angry Mrs. Jones as Tommy realized he was the only one in sight of this upset woman.

"No Ma'am", replied Tommy, "we were all playing

baseball and a hard hit made the ball hit your window", he said. "Well I want to know who is

going to pay for this window?" she said while tossing the ball up and down in her hand. "Who hit the ball?" she asked.

Tommy was stunned at the question. He didn't want to be a snitch on his friend Bobby, but he also knew it was wrong to lie so he wasn't going to do that either. "Mrs. Jones, I can't tell you who hit the ball because I don't want to be called a snitch", he answered truthfully.

Mrs. Jones' voice became angry as she said to him, "well you better tell me or you are going to pay for the window, and I'll call your parents", she quickly said. Tommy didn't know what to do so he simply said he needed time to think about it and would get back to her soon.

As he walked away she shouted after him that he had better get back to her soon or she would call his parents. Her question presented Tommy with a moral dilemma.

MORAL DILEMA

A *dilemma* ("double proposition") is a problem offering two possibilities, neither of which is good to do.

snitch, and have his friend mad at him, or to have to pay for a window that he didn't break. He decided the right thing to do was to talk with his friend Bobby and have him go to Mrs. Jones and tell her he broke her window.

He went to Bobby's house and when Bobby came to

the door, Tommy said, "come on outside Bobby, I need to talk to you." Bobby knew what Tommy probably wanted to talk about but ignored that and started his own conversation.

"Pretty awesome hit I had today", Bobby bragged. "Yeah and it smashed right through Mrs. Jones' window", Tommy interrupted. "It was a great hit Bobby with only one problem", he said, "Mrs. Jones came out and asked me who was going to pay for the window".

"You didn't tell her I did it did you?" he asked. No, but she said if I don't tell her who is responsible she will call my parents and have me pay for it, said Tommy. "All you have to do is tell your parent's that you don't know who did it and that will be the end of it", Bobby replied.

"No, I won't do that", Tommy said, "because that would be bringing me into the wrongdoing by lying to my parents. You need to go to Mrs. Jones and tell her that you did it by accident, and then pay for the window. That's the best way to make this right". Bobby shook his head not liking the suggestion his friend had just made.

"Heck no, I'm not 'gonna do that. She has no idea I was even there, and besides, I don't have any money anyway". Tommy didn't like what Bobby was saying because he was now putting him in a predicament.

(Predicament – a difficult or unpleasant situation)

The boys went back inside Bobby's house and up to his bedroom. "Bobby you are leaving me no choice. I will not lie to my parents, and I will not pay for your mistake. Now she knows that I know who hit the ball and either you tell her you did, or I will have to".

Bobby got up from sitting on his bed and walked toward Tommy saying angrily, "I thought we were best friends, and now you're going to snitch on me? I wouldn't do that to you!"

Tommy quickly responded saying, "You wouldn't have to because I would never put my best friend in a place where he would be responsible for my mistake, and I sure would never tell you to lie to anyone. You know Bobby, right is right and wrong is wrong. It's actually stealing from that woman if you expect her or anybody else to pay for what you did, whether it was an accident or not".

With that, Tommy began to walk out of Bobby's room. As he was going out of the door, he turned to Bobby and said, "You only have a short time to make up your mind, so you'd better hurry. You know what's right to do here Bobby, so please don't make me have to do something I don't want to do", he continued, and then left the house.

Bobby lay down on his bed hoping homework he had to do would take his mind off of this problem, but it didn't. He then tried to figure the whole thing out, thinking he had gotten away with breaking the window, but he knew that was wrong. Then he began to think of the predicament he had put his friend in who would either have to pay for the

window himself, or snitch on a friend.

Next he thought that if he went and admitted to breaking the window, where would he get the money to pay for it? If he borrowed it from his parents, they would know he tried to ditch the responsibility of what he had done, and if he didn't, it would take weeks of his allowance to pay it off. He didn't think that Mrs. Jones was going to wait that long to have her window fixed, so his parents would find out anyway.

He soon knew he had to make things right, and first found Tommy. He approached him and hung his head. "I'm sorry Tommy, I never thought through this until you explained it that way", he said. "You're my best friend and I would never want you to do things that are wrong. It's one of the things I admire about you so much; so do all of the other guys. You always do what's right, and the good of it is always obvious to all of us. I'm not sure where I'm going to get the money to pay for it though, but I guess I'll ask my Dad", he concluded.

Tommy had been thinking about this situation and had come up with an idea. "Look Bobby, we were all involved in the game, and if all of us chipped in a couple of dollars that should cover it don't you think?" he asked. "Why don't you go over to Mrs. Jones house and tell her it was an accident and you're sorry you ran but were just scared about doing it. Meanwhile I'll find the other guys and get them to chip in for the window. Make sure you find out from Mrs. Jones how much it will cost", he said.

Bobby was thankful for his friend coming up with a great idea that seemed fair to everyone. He also felt much better because he was going to make things right about this with everyone's help.

Mrs. Jones was pleased that Bobby came and

confessed that he had hit the ball and told him it would come to twenty-two dollars. Since there were nine players, everyone would have to chip in two and a half dollars.

Tommy was able to get to the other guys who were playing the game with them when the window was broken, and they all agreed that this was a fair way to take care of the problem.

The boys all chipped in their part and Tommy and Bobby took the money over to Mrs. Jones, again apologizing to her. Mrs. Jones was very pleased that the boys had done the right thing, and all was well once again.

MORAL OF THE STORY

The window was broken and leaving Tommy to take the heat was an act of dishonesty. Fortunately Tommy, because of his integrity with the group, was able to convince them all to do the right thing.

Making things right by being honest and accepting responsibility when we do something wrong, whether we meant to or not, will always make us feel better, and build that great and noble trait that people respect – **INTEGRITY!**

CHAPTER TWO
SOCIAL MEDIA NIGHTMARE

Meghan and Susan were neighbors and had been close friends for ten years. As they entered their twelfth year, they both received smart phones from their parents for Christmas. The first thing they both did was to get together to explore the different things they could do with the phones. They downloaded the app (application) to a music package, and then downloaded their favorite songs. Next they discovered how to send e-mails and load addresses.

A mutual friend, Julie, came over one day when they were together, and told them about the Social Media, and particularly about Facebook and Twitter. They eagerly downloaded those apps and began to add friends in both.

Meghan excitedly told her parents about the Social Media she had discovered, and neither of her parents were familiar with them, other than hearing about them once in a while in conversations.

Over a week or so they both seemed to add most of their friends at school to these apps and were having fun texting and sharing everyday events with their friends.

As what usually happens in seventh grade, boys and girls begin noticing the opposite sex and some even had had boyfriends and girlfriends since being in the fifth grade, but those things never seem to last very long, and change quite regularly.

A new boy moved into their neighborhood that was their age and ended up in their class. He was a particularly good-looking boy named Tom Keller, and they both took a liking to him. When they realized they were both interested in Tom, there soon became a competition between them for his attention and things began to heat up between these close friends.

They began to have arguments about who Tom liked more, and even went as far as to calling each other names and making fun of each other. Of course, Tom had no idea any of this was going on as the girls kept their arguing about him to themselves. Soon Tom, who lived on the same street as both girls, began walking home with them after school. They all three became friends, but the competition for Tom continued between the girls without him having any idea about it.

The school was having its annual Thanksgiving Day Festival, where they had the gymnasium filled with different games and booths to raise money for the current school project. Families and students would come and play the games, like throwing a baseball to knock down three bottles stacked up and win a prize. They also had cake walks, ring tosses, face painting, and the like for the fun of the crowd and to raise the money they needed.

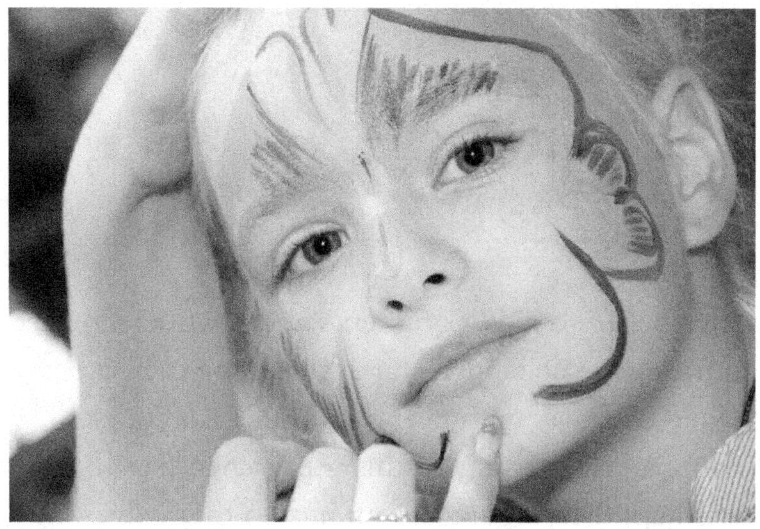

Tom asked Meghan to go to the Festival with him, and Susan was hurt. Since all three had become friends, she saw no reason for Tom not to take them both. The more she thought about it, the more upset she became. Her refusal to understand that Tom may prefer Meghan over her made her mad; in fact she became livid **(livid – furiously angry)**. She didn't realize that her anger was really a result of her feelings being hurt, but she foolishly wanted to hurt back.

As Susan thought more and more about the situation, she kept focusing on untruths like Meghan had purposely arranged this, or that Tom was being fooled by Meghan going after him so that Susan wouldn't have a chance with a relationship with Tom and so on, and so on. Her jealousy of Meghan became so strong that she began to think of ways to hurt her back. Meghan did nothing to hurt Susan purposely, nor did she realize that all of this was going on with her best friend, because Susan was hiding her feelings. Susan decided to make up a disparaging story.

(*Disparaging – to describe someone or something as unimportant, weak, bad, and hurt their reputation)

about Meghan and post it on her social media. She made up the story that Meghan was a shop-lifter who stole from the local stores, and then posted it on her social media to her friends. She never realized that once posted you can't take it back, and that the damage caused can be forwarded to many more people who were friends of her friends.

When someone lies, they find out usually that one lie leads to another, and another as questions are asked. Soon Susan's friends began to ask Susan if this was true, and she had to lie and say yes to keep herself from looking bad for posting this untruth. Many of them were surprised, not only because Meghan was Susan's best friend, but because of that, they were surprised that Susan would post it about Meghan.

As the story gained momentum, Susan began to realize that she had really done something terrible. She also began to realize that when the truth came out it would be her reputation that would be ruined because of all of the lies, especially making up such a story about her friend.

Well, it didn't take long for this to get back to Meghan. Even though Susan had made sure she did not send the post to Meghan, she began to hear about it from everyone else. At first she thought it was a joke someone had started, until one of the girls pulled her phone out and showed Meghan the post by Susan.

Looking at the untruthful post had a numbing effect on Meghan. Then, as the reality of how many people were now seeing this about her and not knowing it is a lie, it began to sink in. Meghan was crushed to her very soul to know that her best friend had stooped so low as to publish this terrible untruth about her. She went home in despair and locked herself in her room crying.

Her parents knocked on her door asking to be let in, so she opened the door. They asked her what was wrong, and she began to tell them what had happened. Her father became quite angry at first, but after calming down he told Meghan he was going to speak to Susan's father about this.

He went downstairs and as he opened the front door, he found Susan and her father getting ready to knock. Susan's father asked if they could come in and Meghan's dad told them of course. Susan was clinging to her father and sobbing because she had realized how this must have hurt her best friend and was afraid to face her.

Meghan's dad asked them to have a seat in the living room and went upstairs to see if Meghan wanted to come down to hear what they had to say. Meghan had let her hair down and was brushing it when her dad came in the room. At first she said no, and then decided it had to be done sooner or later so she went with her dad.

As they entered their living-room, Susan put her head down in shame and was afraid to look at Meghan. Susan's father began to say that his daughter had come to him about this horrible thing she had done and wanted to do whatever she could to correct the matter.

He explained that he knew very little about this social media stuff but had figured out that a posted confession by his daughter about her lies would be a good start. He furthered stated that he had taken her smart phone, and she would not get it back until she was much older and could understand the damage these things can cause to people.

Susan looked up and caught Meghan's eyes. She began to cry saying, "Meggie I am so sorry for all that I did and have no excuse at all. I was jealous that Tom asked you to go to the festival with him and felt hurt and wanted to get back at you for something that was never your fault. Can you ever forgive me?"

It turns out that Meghan had recently had a Sunday school class at church about the importance of forgiveness, and it had really made an impression on her. She stood up and said sternly, "Susan you need to post the confession about all of this right away, and make sure you confess to people asking about the lies you told."

Susan realizing that it looked like Meghan wasn't going to forgive her just lowered her head and said, "of course I will". Then, surprisingly to Susan, Meghan said, "And of course I will forgive you, you're my best friend and we all make mistakes. With that Susan ran to Meghan sobbing, and they hugged each other, Susan kept saying how sorry she was while Meghan said, "I know, I know".

Meghan's dad sat back with a very proud look on his face for his daughter's decision, while Meghan and

Susan went running up the stairs to Meghan's bedroom to discuss other events going on in their lives.

The best friends were reunited through the power of forgiveness, and another of life's hard lessons was learned. If you lie in a way that hurts people, it will never go away until resolved.

MORAL OF THE STORY

Untruths, better known as lies, can not only hurt and damage the person being lied about, but usually end up causing lie after lie to cover up the first one. This will hurt and damage the liar much more than the victim of the original lie.

Forgiveness for lying may not come as easy or at all as it did in Meghan and Susan's story, and even if it does come, there are usually harsh consequences to the liar.

CHAPTER THREE
THE STORY TELLER

Bill Cook was a boy who grew up feeling lonely. Maybe he felt that way because it seemed like he was not getting much attention from his parents, and others seemed to ignore him due to his shyness. As he grew older he was always making up stories that weren't true for the purpose of getting some attention. Some of his stories were quite unbelievable, and when found out to be not true, he gained the reputation of nothing but a story teller.

His story telling began at age four when he would call for his mother in an urgent tone and tell her things like there were animals under his bed, or he had seen someone in his closet, or a bear was in the backyard.

Once in school Bill felt left out on the playground and with the neighborhood kids. The main reason was Bill's shyness causing him to stay to himself, or mostly on the sidelines of the kids' activities. He wanted to participate with the other kids but didn't know how to go about it, so he found himself continually watching from afar.

Bill decided the way to get some attention was to make up things the other boys would be interested in and try to have them get involved with him in looking into them. He never thought about what would happen when they found out he was lying.

One day, several of his classmates in his neighborhood were in a vacant lot throwing the football around. Bill went running up to them telling them he had just seen a small alligator in the area of the creek where the water pooled. This small pool the creek formed made a good swimming hole in the summer for the kids.

They all began with the "you did not, and no way"

sayings until they saw the excitement Bill was showing. Then it was "let's go" as they all caught on to the excitement of the story, and began to run down the street, through the field and down the hill to the creek. They then ran down along the creek to the area where the water created a deeper pool where they had their swimming hole. They excitedly asked Bill where he had seen it and was it on the shore or in the water.

Bill quickly said that he had seen it floating along in the swimming hole. With that the questions began, "Well where exactly?", and "can they stay under water long?", and "where do you think it is?" Jimmy and Dan picked up some rocks and began throwing them into the swimming hole area trying to bring it to the surface. Sam got a long stick and started prodding the water. Jimmy said, "Are you sure it was an Alligator?" Bill shook his head yes. "How big was it?" asked Sam. "I don't know, maybe ten feet long", Bill answered. "Ten feet long, give me a break", said Dan. "If it was that big we would sure be able to see it in this shallow hole", said Jimmy.

The boys began to realize that Bill was not telling the truth about this whole thing, and they became annoyed with him. "What are you trying to prove with this phony story?" asked Dan. "Yeah, why did you bring us down here with this lie?" Jimmy said. "Maybe it got away", Bill tried to suggest, attempting to get himself out of this big whopper of a story.

With that the three boys turned and left Bill and headed back to the vacant lot. On the way they talked about what was wrong with Bill to tell such a tale, and made comments about what a jerk he was, and wondered why he was always making up stories that were never true.

Bill felt bad at what he had done, and just couldn't believe he had made up such a story. He walked home wondering what he was going to do about this big lie, and how he was going to get out of what he had told the guys.

The next day in school the boys ignored him even more, and when they did make eye contact, they just sort of shook their heads and then went on about what they were doing. Bill realized he had really done it this time, and just stayed to himself.

Every once in a while one of the boys would ask him if he had seen anymore alligators lately. Any of the other classmates in earshot would ask what alligators, and they would tell the story giving Bill a bad reputation for his lie. Bill went on for weeks feeling very sad about his doing this, and thinking he was never going to get out of it, or even that the boys would just finally let it pass.

One late spring day, Bill was back down at the creek by himself walking along the water when he heard a cry for help. He looked down the creek and the little rope bridge that had been there for years had broken, and a girl in her teens was laying in the creek, half in and half out of the water.
The rope bridge had broken when she was crossing, and she fell a short fall but hit her head on one of the rocks and was very woozy. "Help me", she said faintly to Bill as he ran to where she was. Bill tried to

take her arms and pull her out of the water but didn't have the strength to get her out. "Please help me, I can't move", she pleaded with Bill as he was trying to decide what to do.

"I'll be right back with help", Bill said to her, "It'll be alright, I'll be right back", he continued as he then got up and ran for help. Bill was very scared for the girl as he saw some blood on her head and didn't know how bad she was.

Bill's parents weren't at home and he knew he had to find some help fast. As he ran up the hill, through the field and down the road he saw some of the boys in the vacant lot throwing a baseball. He ran up to the lot and saw it was Jimmy, Dan, and Sam that were playing ball. Bill ran up to them and excitedly said, "Guys, quick come with me, there's a girl hurt down at the creek. The rope bridge broke and she fell and hit her head on a rock", he said breathlessly from the running.

"Yeah, right and I suppose the alligator is about to eat her too", said Sam as he obviously didn't believe a word of it. "Don't you ever learn?" asked Jimmy completely skeptical of what he was being told. Still trying to catch his breath Bill said, "No, really, I'm not lying; she is hurt, and I tried to pull her on to the bank but couldn't". "She is bleeding from her head and said she can't move. You've got to believe me", he hurriedly told them in a panic to get the girl some help. Dan noticed something different in Bill's

(demeanor – a person's appearance or behavior)

demeanor and said, "Wait a minute, I think he's telling the truth". Both the other boys looked at him and said, "Ok, but if this is another one of your whopper's you're going to pay for it".

They all four began the run back down the road, across the field and down the hill to the creek. They quickly found the young teen girl just as Bill had said. "Quick, let's get her out of the water and on to the grass", Bill said taking control. "Jimmy put your sweater over her to try and keep her warm, and I'll run back up and get someone to call the paramedics", Bill said now handling the situation well. "You guys stay with her till I get back", Bill said.

Bill was very tired for making the run to the guys and back, but his adrenaline was flowing with the danger of the situation, and he just ran as fast as he could to get help.

(Adrenaline - a substance that is released in the body of a person who is feeling a strong emotion (such as excitement, fear, or anger) and that causes the heart to beat faster and gives the person more energy)

Bill was gone about fifteen minutes as he had caught one of the neighbors in her yard and had her call 911 for help, and then ran back down after directing the neighbor where to send the paramedics. The boys could hear the siren in the distance and knew help was on the way.

The paramedics arrived soon and began checking the girl's injuries. First they put a brace around her neck to stabilize it from moving, then cleaned and put a bandage on her cut head to stop the bleeding.

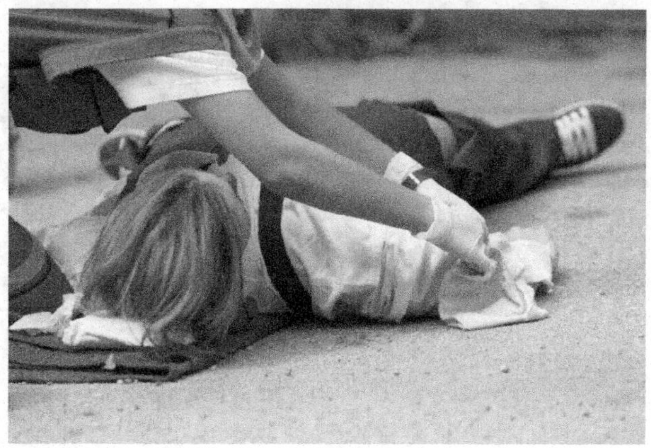

They finally checked her legs which she told them she couldn't move.

Fortunately, they had brought a body basket with them, and carefully and slowly lifted her into it. The two paramedics then got on each side of her and lifted the basket while starting a slow run for the ambulance.

The boys ran ahead leading the way back, to where there was now a small crowd of people trying to see what was going on. Some policemen arrived as well as a fire truck, and there was even a news truck there. The crowd began to clap to let the paramedics know their gratitude for such quick service.

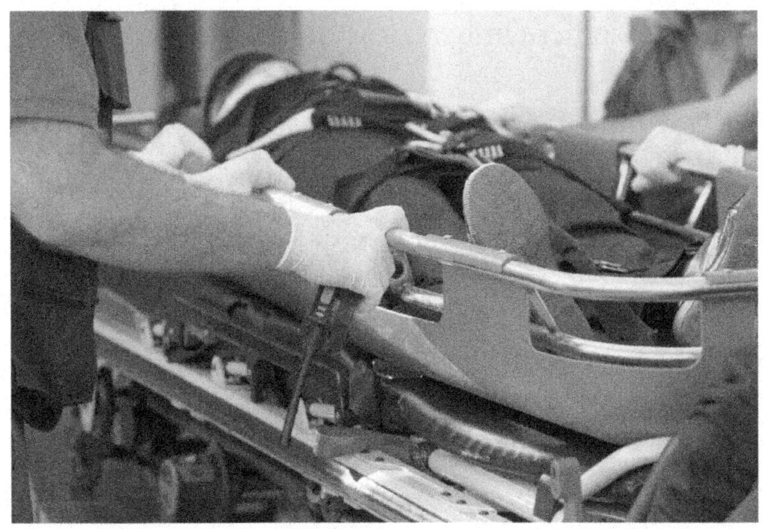

They slowly lifted the girl into the ambulance, and she asked to see Bill. "Thank you, ahh", "Bill" said Bill as she was trying to know his name. "Yes, thank you Bill, you may have saved my life", she said, as the paramedics closed the door of the ambulance and headed down the street with the siren and lights flashing.

The boys were ecstatic about what had happened and their place in helping rescue the teen girl. "Wow Bill, you sure handled that great", said Jimmy. "You're not kidding", said Dan, "you really did a great job". "Thanks", said Bill, "And thanks for believing me after that last episode. I don't know what caused me to tell such a big lie, but I'm sorry".

"That's Ok dude, you are forgiven", said Dan. About that time the local news people came up to the boys and asked them what had happened. The other boys were quick to point out that if it hadn't been for Bill, she might still be down there. They asked Bill on camera about his heroism in saving the girl, and he simply said, "I could have never done it without the help of my friends here", as he stood with Jimmy, Dan and Sam. "We did it together", Bill stated, as they all four turned and walked on back down the road together.

MORAL OF THE STORY

It never pays to make up stories and lies about things. Once others hear them and find out they are not true, you can be labeled a liar and no one wants to hear any more from you. Then, when something serious happens it is difficult to get anyone to believe you, which could end up very badly.

Here, Bill was able to convince his friends to help him before it was too late. If they had walked away from him what might have happened to the hurt girl in cold water?

CHAPTER FOUR
ALWAYS BIGGER AND BETTER

Gary Adkins was a boy that always seemed to be in trouble. One of the reasons was he would lie about everything and anything to get attention or attempt to keep himself out of trouble. Whenever anyone would talk about something they did, he had also done it, and more, bigger and better than the person telling the story.

Carol Grant was in Gary's class, and one day for an exercise, their teacher Mrs. Hearsom, asked if

that they did over the Spring break. Several raised

their hands and Carol was picked to tell her story. Carol stood up and was asked to come to the front of the class. She began about the Cockatiel bird her parents had bought her, and how these birds could talk. She explained that it really takes working with them regularly before they can learn a word or two, but she had managed to teach Dimple, her bird's name, several words over the break.

One thing she taught him was to say "Kiss Carol and make the kissing sound. Now he would say it every time she entered her room like, "Kiss Carol, Kiss Carol, nch, nch, nch, nch, nch". She went on to say that she was teaching him to crow like a rooster, but so far he sounds like a car motor trying to start, "r-r-ra, r-r-r-a, r-r-ra", she mimicked. All the kids laughed, and Carol took her seat.

Gary raised his hand, and as the teacher called on him, he blurted out that he had taught his bird all kinds of things, and that it took him no time at all. "Well that's great Gary, what kind of bird do you have", she commented. He had to think fast as he didn't know the names of most birds and he couldn't remember what Carol had called hers.

"It's a parrot", he said quickly. Mrs. Hearsom asked him if he wanted to tell the class what he had taught the parrot, but he just said, "Well lots of stuff, you know the things people usually train parrots to say", he began, not having any idea what people train parrots to say.

A number of his classmates had been to Gary's house and knew he was lying. Several of them sort of mumbled under their breath's things like, "Yeah, right", or "You liar". Mrs. Hearsom asked them if they had something to say to which they answered, "No Ma'am". "Ok, then keep quiet", she said.

"Ring" went the bell ending class for the day and saving Gary from a very embarrassing situation. Now the main problem with this story was not only that Gary had never taught his parrot to speak, but that he had no parrot at all. Also when school got out the lies got worse. Hal and Larry, the two boys making the comments in class came up to Gary and said, "What a liar, you don't have a parrot!" Gary responded, "Yes I do, how would you know anyway? "Did you forget we've been to your house?" asked Larry. "You guys haven't been over in a couple of weeks, and we got the parrot since then", exclaimed Gary. "Oh really", said Hal, "Well let's all go over and see it, and you can show us what you taught it". "Well I'd like to, but I have a dentist appointment right now after school, and I've got to be going", Gary said as he turned from the boys and headed out.

Gary had no parrot and was telling a bold face lie to his teacher and class, and he also lied about teaching it words in a short time to make it sound like he was better than Carol in teaching her bird. He then repeated both lies when his classmates approached him outside about it, and then lied to their face about having a dentist appointment in order to get out of taking them to his house to show them something that was not there. Gary got home and went into his room and tried to think of a way out of it. He realized he could only buy some time with more lies, but eventually his classmates would find out the truth.

MORAL DILEMA

The consequences for bold face lies are that you have to tell more lies to cover the last one. They have to end somewhere because the teller will either get caught or must be smart and apologize for telling such whoppers, ending the lying in the proper way.

The first thing he did was ask his parents at dinner if they could get a parrot for a pet. "I'll take care of it, and even teach it to talk", he said. His mother replied, "Oh no, birds are very messy and require a lot of attention, and I don't have the time!" "No Mom, I said I will take care of it", Gary replied. "Oh sure you will, when it's convenient for you, then it falls on me", she said.

"Gary, it doesn't matter because parrots are hundreds of dollars, and we don't have that kind of money for any bird, now or ever", his Dad chimed in.

Gary now saw that his bright idea to get himself out of his mess with lying was not going to work. He kept on thinking about it, and finally realized what he was going to have to do to get things straight. He realized that it was going to be very difficult for him, but it was the only way.

The next day he went up to the teacher before class, and hem hawed around trying to get the words out.

(Hem Haw – to pause a lot, and avoid saying something directly)

He finally told her that he had lied about the parrot story and was sorry. "I don't know why I said what I did, but I did and I'm sorry", he told her. His teacher looked at him with compassion and

(Compassion - sympathetic <u>consciousness</u> of others' distress together with a desire to alleviate it)

said, "Gary maybe the reason you always seem to have a bigger and better story than others is that you think it will make you look better to those who hear it. You should know that is not true", she explained. "All that does is make people think that anything you have to say is a lie", she continued.

"You know Gary, you have a lot on the ball, and you don't need to make up stories to have people like you. Just be yourself and you will do just fine", she concluded. She went on to tell him that she accepted his apology, but he had lied to the whole class, and would need to tell them also. He knew she was going to say that, and didn't want to do it, but had decided he needed to get out from under the weight of the lies he had told.

The bell rang and Mrs. Hearsom said, "Class, Gary has something to say to you". Gary, still at the teacher's desk looked out above the class and said, "I want to apologize for telling you that I had a parrot I had taught words to", he began. "I don't have a parrot and I'm not sure why I said I did". He continued, "Carol, I'm sorry I tried to try to outdo your story, and Hal and Larry I'm sorry I continued that after school".

Gary's knees where shaking as he started back to his seat. Mrs. Hearsom told the class, "even though Gary should never have told these lies, it takes a big person to stand up and admit he has done wrong. I hope you will all forgive him". In order to get the air cleared quickly for Gary, she continued right away, "Ok take out your history books, and turn to page 103".

MORAL OF THE STORY

Bold face lies are told when people know they are not true. Gary had told his lie without thinking about his class friends who had recently been to his house and knew he didn't have a parrot. When they approached him, he had to make up another lie to cover the first, and so on. Telling the truth is the only way in life to keep straight and morally sound.

CHAPTER FIVE
NEVER ADMITTED DOING WRONG

Jenny Traver could never understand why no one ever seemed to want to be around her. She was just like the other kids who liked video games, texting, ice skating, and playing softball, but no one ever called her; she had to call and invite herself along. It was Saturday in the winter, and the school had a small skating rink where many of the people in the neighborhood liked to go and do some ice skating. The night before, it had snowed an inch or so, and the ice would have to be shoveled to make the skating better.

Early Saturday morning, Jill Linder, one of the girls in Jenny's class took her shovel and went on her own to shovel the snow off of the skating area behind the school. It took her an hour or so, and when she was done she was cold and tired and went home to warm up and get some breakfast.

Ice skating was popular in this northern Ohio town during the winter, and about ten-thirty people began to show up, some with shovels expecting to have to remove the snow before skating. Jenny was one of the first to show up, and when the others got there and saw the snow already shoveled to the side, they asked Jenny if she did it. "Yeah", said Jenny, "I came early to clear it off so we could all skate". "Well great, thanks for the hard work. We were going to

do it but it's sure nice that it's done already" said one of the guys who had brought his shovel.

After Jill had her breakfast, she put her skates over her shoulders and headed back to the school rink. By that time a number of people were there, and one of her friends Karen, told her that Jenny had shoveled the snow earlier to clear the ice.

Jenny didn't know who had done the shoveling when she took credit for it, and when Karen told Jill that Jenny had done it, she was angry. Jill said to Karen, "She did not! I came early to clear the snow, and there was no one else here to help me. After I got done I was cold and hungry, so I went home to warm up and get some breakfast".

The two girls both looked at Jenny in disgust, and instead of Jenny owning up and admitting she lied, she simply said, "Oh so what, get over it!" and went on skating like nothing had happened at all. She was completely unrepentant for her lie.

(unrepentant – showing no regret for one's wrongdoings)

Jill was not surprised that Jenny didn't own up to her lying, because she had had more of her lying situations before, and Jenny never apologized for anything when she would get caught. Her favorite expression was always, "Oh get over it", and then just going on like nothing ever happened.

The next day, Linda Johnson, a girl living across the street saw Jenny, and went out to talk with her. "Jenny did you know that Bo Hendricks took his Mom's car and drove it around the block while his parents were out shopping the other day?" she asked. Now Jenny didn't know a thing about it but answered, "Oh sure I did, and I happened to be with him when he did". "You were?" asked Linda who was quite skeptical having known of many lies Jenny had told before.

(Skeptical - not easily convinced; having doubts or reservations)

Linda made a bad decision and decided to bait Jenny to try and have her caught in her lie.

(bait – to attract or catch)

"Did you also know he got caught and was grounded for a month by his father?" Linda asked. "Yeah, I knew that, tough luck for him", Linda replied. "Well at least his parents are going to let his friends see him at his house", Linda continued with her ruse.

(Ruse -a trick or act that is used to fool someone)

"Great, I think I'll go and see him", Jenny said.

Moral Dilemma – it is never right to use one lie to correct another. "Two wrongs never make a right" Linda was wrong in doing this.

On the way to Bo's house Jenny thought she would try to get Bo to tell others that she was with him when he drove his parent's car. She knew if he would, it would cover her lie to Linda.

Jenny arrived at Bo's house and knocked on the door. Bo's Dad came to the door and Jenny said, "I heard that Bo was grounded for driving his Mom's car around the block the other day, and I just wanted to see if I could see him to cheer him up".

Bo's Dad looked at Jenny in unbelief. Just as he was about to say something Bo walked up from the side yard. He had been out sledding on the big hill at the end of the neighborhood and was coming home for lunch. "Hi Jenny", Bo said not realizing what was going on.

"Bo's Dad looked at Bo and said, "It seems that Jenny heard you were grounded for taking Mom's car around the block while we were gone the other day". With that, Bo's countenance changed quickly.

(Countenance – a person's facial expression)

"Well, I, uh, I mean that", he started to say. Jenny realized that she had really done it now with all of her lying.

"Well, I can see from your reaction we have something to talk about", his Dad said. "Driving at twelve years old is unlawful and unacceptable. You are in real trouble", his Dad continued. "Get in this house", his dad commanded. Bo dropped the rope to his sled and looked at Jenny with an evil stare, as he walked past his Dad and into the house.

"Who told you this?" Bo's Dad asked Jenny. "Linda Moore" came Jenny's quick response. "Ok, I'll be speaking with her parents", Bo's Dad said as he closed the door. Jenny knew this was going to turn out bad.

After Bo's Dad spoke to Linda's parents, and they had found out from Linda that she told the truth about Bo driving the car, but later lied to Jenny to get her in trouble, they punished her. "Lying is never acceptable", Linda's father told her. "But Jenny lies all of the time and always seems to get away with it. I wanted to teach her a lesson", replied Linda to her Dad.

“It’s not your place to teach Jenny a lesson”, said her father. “Now look what’s happened, he continued, “Bo may be getting what he deserved for doing such a foolish thing, but now you’re grounded for lying”. “Yeah, and Jenny gets away with her lies again”, Linda complained.

In the meantime, Jenny had decided she needed to head off the trouble she thought was coming. She went to her parents and lied to them about the situation. “Believe me I had nothing to do with this at all, she said to her parents.

Unfortunately for Jenny, her Dad was best friends with Linda’s Dad. He called Linda’s Dad and found out about all of the lying going on by both girls, and confronted Jenny about it.

“Mr. Johnson told me the whole story Linda”, he began, “about how she baited you with a lie about Bo being caught and grounded for his driving”, he continued, “and Linda told her dad the reason she tried to trap you was because you are always lying, and always getting away with it. Well no more, you’re grounded for a month and I’ll decide what else you’re going to get”, her dad finished.

"No, he's lying Dad, I had nothing to do with this", she claimed again. "Ok Jenny, Linda's Dad is now lying. Do you expect me to believe that? You are grounded without cell phone or TV", said Jenny's Dad, "for not owning up to what you did. And if I hear of or catch you lying again, there will be more severe consequences! Do you understand me young lady?" he asked.

Without waiting for his daughter to respond he said, "Jenny you'd better realize that no one wants to be around a liar. People know they can't trust a liar, and if they can't trust you, they will never want to be your friend", her Dad said, "and you'll be left out." "I didn't do anything wrong", Jenny insisted. "Well, you better think about that before it's too late", her Dad said, as he picked up her cell phone and closed the door of her room.

Back in school word got around about Jenny even lying to her dad and never admitting she had done wrong. As a result, her classmates would have nothing to do with her. Jenny became isolated.

(Isolated – separate from others)

She just couldn't seem to understand what the big deal was because she lied a little bit.

MORAL OF THE STORY

Would you want to be a friend or around someone you couldn't trust? Jenny was an unrepentant liar in that she would never admit she had lied or done wrong. As a result, she was punished, and should have had the answer to her earlier question of why it seemed no one wanted to be around her. When a person begins lying, they find they have to lie repeatedly to cover up the last lie. Eventually they will get caught and face consequences.

CHAPTER SIX
BACKED INTO A CORNER

Kerry Peters was an eleven year old boy and well-liked by his friends and classmates. He had a great personality and always seemed to get along with everyone. He was on the honor role in his sixth grade class and helped out with the bulletin boards in his room to assist his teacher, Mrs. Kraft.

“Kerry, after math tomorrow, will you help me get the Spring bulletin boards up?” she asked. “I have some cut-outs I have put together to decorate the boards for Spring, and I could sure use your help”, she said. “Sure, I’d be glad to. I’m just finishing up the one for science class”, he replied. “Thank you, you always do such a good job. I really appreciate it”, she said.

Kerry went home that afternoon and threw the football with his older brother, and then they went in for dinner. He did his homework after dinner and watched some television before going to bed.

The next day after math class, Kerry went and got the materials from Mrs. Kraft and began working on the bulletin boards. He was using the big pair of sharp scissors to cut out a large picture he was going to put up. The big scissors were awkward to use and very sharp but worked well to cut out the big pictures and saved a lot of time.

He was working on the large bulletin board that was alongside the coat rack built into the wall. Kerry was lost in his work and wasn't paying attention when he swung around, and the large scissors slipped and made a gash in James Readings new leather coat that he got last Christmas. His first reaction was one of guilt for the coat being damaged, but it was just an accident. He slowly looked around and no one seemed to have seen what had happened to the coat. Kerry knew how much James like that leather coat and became afraid to tell him he made the gash in it.

He continued finishing up the bulletin board quickly and then put everything away, taking his seat like nothing had happened. The bell rang for the end of classes, and everyone put their things away and went to get their coats. James didn't notice the gash at first, and he swung the coat around his shoulders while putting it on.

"Hey James, what happened to your coat", asked Will Benson who had noticed the gash in his sleeve. "What do you mean?" asked James, "What gash?" Then as Will pointed to his sleeve, he looked down and saw it. It was about three inches long on his left sleeve, and he was upset. "What the heck happened to that", he asked unsuspectingly.

Some of the boys in including Kerry gathered around James as he said, "Well I sure didn't do it. I'd have known about catching it on something, or feel it tear", he stated. "Great, now my parents are going to be upset with me thinking I was careless with it", he said.

"Do any of you guys know what happened?" he asked the group around him. "I sure don't know", said Will, "I can't imagine what happened." "Hey Kerry, you were working over by where James' coat was hanging", said Chuck, another of the boys in the group, "Did you see anything?"

MORAL DILEMMA – answering that he knew now would make Kerry look bad because he had never told James right when it happened as he should have. Now he felt backed into a corner.

Kerry felt like he was cornered and was confused about what to do. He hadn't done it purposely and it was an accident he couldn't foresee; however an expensive coat of his good friend had been damaged by him and he had to make a decision. He couldn't believe what came out of his mouth next.

"No, I didn't see anything. I was too busy putting up the cut-outs Mrs. Kraft had given me", he said, but not without looking somewhat guilty. Kerry was a good guy, but he failed to tell the truth because it would make him look bad. However, his body language was making it look like he knew more than he was saying.

(body language - can include body posture, gestures, facial expressions, and eye movements that can give away clues)

"Kerry, why do you look like that?" asked James sort of laughing, "you almost look like you did it"; James said without a thought that Kerry had done it. Kerry was a good friend of James, and James never suspected Kerry might have done it for a moment. "Well, I know my folks are not going to be happy when I get home and they see this", said James, as he started out of the classroom door with the guys following him; that is all but Kerry.

Kerry remained back and was fighting within himself how to correct this terrible mistake he had made by not telling the truth. He was very troubled, but he remembered what his Father had always taught him, that honesty was the best policy. He finally decided what he had to do. "Hey, wait up you guys", Kerry yelled after the other boys and he ran to catch up with them, then he reached out for James's arm getting him to stop.

"James, I accidently cut your coat when I was working on the bulletin boards", he began. "I was using those big scissors, and as I turned they slipped hitting the sleeve of your coat gashing it. I'm so sorry I didn't tell you when it happened, but I know how much you love that coat, and I was, well just afraid to tell you what I had done", he confessed. "I don't know what got into me, but I'm sure sorry". Kerry finished.

James looked at Kerry for ten seconds or so, which felt like a year to Kerry, then said, "Well you've done the right thing now, as you usually do, so stop worrying about it. I forgive you", James said.

"Now you'll probably have to come up with a way to pay for the repair, but it'll be Ok", he said putting his arm around his friend. "You know we all make mistakes", James said to Kerry and the other guys, "and the best way to deal with mistakes is to own up and fix the situation".

Kerry was glad to have such a good friend as James and knew he would never be reluctant to tell the truth again.

MORAL OF THE STORY

Even the best of people can or have lied when their backs were up against the wall, so to speak. Always telling the truth is the best policy, and if we lie, we should go and correct the lie with the truth quickly. Otherwise the situation can only get worse, and much harder to deal with.

CHAPTER SEVEN
THEY NEVER HURT ANYONE UNTIL…

Samantha's Mother had recently lost some weight and had just come home from shopping for some clothes for herself that would fit better. She and Samantha's Dad had an important party they were going to, and she wanted to look her best.

Samantha walked into her Mother's room while she was trying on clothes. Her Mother saw her and asked, "What do you think about this one Sam?" as she held the dress in front of her before the mirror. "I don't know, what you think?" was the response from Sam who didn't like the look of the dress for her Mother at all. "I like it, or of course I wouldn't have bought it", said her mother. "What do you think?" she again asked Sam in hopes of getting a positive response.

Samantha realized her Mother had just spent money on this dress, and although she didn't like it, she decided to give her mother what she wanted. "Oh, I think its great Mom", said Samantha. "Do you really", asked her mother again. "Yeah Mom, it looks great", answered Samantha. "Well I got to go over to Judy's house for a while", said Samantha as she walked out of her mother's room. "Ok, but don't be late for dinner", her mother yelled after her.

As Samantha headed over to Judy's, she felt kind of bad because she told her mother a lie about her dress, when he mother wanted her honest opinion. Oh well, she thought, it was only a little white lie.

MORAL DILEMMA

Being truthful is the only way to build one's integrity. "Little White Lies" are untruths and may come back with consequences.

When Samantha got to Judy's house, they went out on the back patio to talk. Samantha began to tell Judy about the lousy looking dress her mother had bought for a party, and that she lied to her when she had asked what she thought about it.

"I feel bad that I wasn't honest with Mom", said Samantha. "I should have told her the truth about my opinion". "Oh Sam, you're so square, it's no big deal to lie about things like that", Judy said.

Samantha knew many people who felt like that, and called it "Little White Lies", but somehow she knew it was wrong, and couldn't seem to shake the bad feeling about it, even with Judy's comments.

Just then Judy's mother called out to Judy and asked, "What are you two doing out there?" Her mother needed help moving a big bookcase in the living room, but Judy just thought she was checking on them. "We're right in the middle of coming up with a science project Mom", Judy called back. "Oh okay", her mother said turning back to the living room.

Samantha knew Judy had just lied to her Mom about something that also seemed like no big deal. As the two girls continued to talk, they heard a loud noise and then Judy's mother yelling in pain. Both girls jumped up and ran inside.

Judy's mother was on the floor with the top of the full bookcase on her foot, and it was obvious she was in real pain. "Mom, what happened", she asked in a panic. Her mother answered in pain filled words, "I was trying to move the bookcase over a few inches, and the top section slipped off and hit my foot".

"Mom, why were you doing that yourself? Why didn't you ask us to help?" Judy asked. "Well I tried, but after finding out you two were in the middle of a science project, I thought I could do it myself without bothering you", answered her mother.

Judy and Samantha were both stung by her mother's answer. Judy had lied to her mother, just a little white lie that had now caused this painful injury to her mother. Judy began to cry as she could see the pain her mother was in and blamed herself for the problem. "Oh Mom, I'm sorry, we could've helped, we were just fooling around outside" she sobbed, "we weren't working on a science project, I thought you were just checking on us", she said. 'Well don't think about it now", her mother said, "Call your Dad and ask him to come get me and take me to the emergency room", she said while trying fight the pain.

Judy ran to her phone and called her Dad, who was there in fifteen minutes. He carefully helped his wife to the car and took her to the doctor. Judy's mother had a small cut and a broken bone in her foot but was alright.

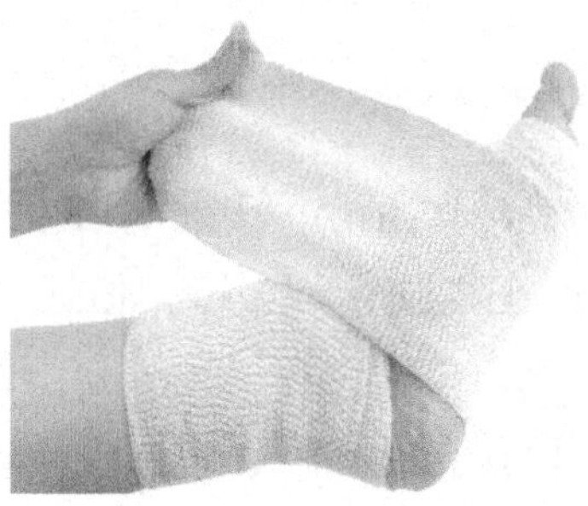

When her parents came home she apologized for the lie, and her Dad explained to her that any untruth, no matter how "White" it may be, can result in consequences that are hurtful. He made sure his daughter understood she was always to tell the truth.

Samantha went home and apologized to her mother. "Mom, I'm sorry I lied to you when I told you I liked your dress. I thought it was just a little white lie in not wanting to hurt your feelings but have since become aware that the truth is always the best way to go. Please forgive me".

"I do forgive you Sam, and you're right, no matter whatever the situation is, always be truthful. If you are worried about hurting someone's feelings, you can tell the truth in different ways", her mother continued. "You could have said something like Mom, that wouldn't be my first choice, which would convey your feeling without lying", she explained. "Sam, you can always find the right thing to say without having to lie. Just remember there is no such thing as a white lie, only a lie" her mother told her. "Thanks Mom, I understand and have learned a good lesson today".

MORAL OF THE STORY

Judy learned the hard way why telling any kind of lie, even what seems like a small one, can have serious consequences you can't foresee. Sam had her bad feeling about her lie confirmed when she saw what happened to Judy's mother.

CHAPTER EIGHT
LYING TO MY PARENTS IS NO BIG DEAL

Craig Dalton and his friend Joe Fisher were on their way out of the house one afternoon, when his mother met them at the front door. "Craig where do you think you are going", his mother asked him. "Oh just down to play some "hoops" Mom", was his quick response. "No sir mister, you have not done your chores yet, and they will all be done before you go anywhere", she commanded. "Mom, I finished my chores already, and I have to go because our game is about to start", he said. "You're telling me all of your chores were done in the last hour, because they weren't before that?" she asked him. "Yeah mom, all done", he said. "We'll you wait here while I check", Mrs. Dalton told him. Just then the phone rang, and Craig's mom began talking to her best friend, and just waived Craig on, so off they went.

"Well that was easier than I thought", said Craig as he and Joe ran out and across the field. As they got far enough away and slowed down, Joe said to Craig, "I can't believe you just lied to your Mother. What's

going to happen when she finds out?" he asked. "Oh Mom will probably forget about it after her call. It's usually Dad who checks on jobs being done, and he's out of town", Craig responded. "Man, if I lied to my parents I wouldn't see daylight for two weeks", Joe told Craig.

The two boys arrived at the park where their other friends were shooting basketball until they got there. "What took you so long?" Jimmy asked. "I had to do my chores before I could get out", said Craig. Joe just looked at Craig in amazement as he had just told another lie. "Oh you didn't do your chores", Joe said, contradicting his friend. "Yeah, well I had to make it seem like I did so I could get here on time", retorted Craig, annoyed that Joe had given his lie away.

Sides were chosen and the game began, with Craig and Joe on different teams. During the game, Craig was trying to take the ball from a boy on the other

team and the other boy outmaneuvered him. As that boy, Frank, passed the ball to a teammate, Craig shoved him so hard he fell and scraped his knee. Everyone stopped to see what happened.

"What do you think you're doing", said Frank, "that's a foul and you did it on purpose". "Oh I did not", Craig responded, "you just fell". The boy jumped up and shoved Craig saying, "You're a liar.

You did that on purpose because I slipped around you when you went for the ball", said Frank. "You're full of it", Craig said back loudly.

Jimmy came up to both boys and said, "He's not full of it Dalton, we all saw it and you did shove him down on purpose", he said. "Yeah, well if he can't take a little hard B-ball, maybe he shouldn't play", retorted Craig. "No, if you can't play fairly and take the blame when you do something wrong maybe you shouldn't play", said Jimmy right back at him. "OK, Joe you saw it, tell them I didn't shove him down", said Craig.

MORAL DILEMMA

Joe had just been asked by his close friend Craig to lie for him to cover his lie. Joe was respected among his friends for his honesty and was not going to have a friend make him a liar also.

"Craig don't bring me into this", his friend warned. "No, you saw it so tell them what happened", Craig said, expecting his friend to back up his lie. "Alright Craig, I'll tell what I saw. When Frank pulled around you while you were trying to get the ball and got away from you, you ran up and shoved him to the ground, that's what I saw", said Joe reluctantly.

Craig drew back in disbelief. He had been sure his close friend would back him up, but he didn't. He spoke out in anger, "Joe what makes you so lily white all of the time. I suppose you never do anything wrong", Craig asked. No Craig, it's not that I don't do things wrong sometimes, it's that I own up to them when I do", responded Joe. "Now you want me to lie for you to cover your lie, and I'm not going to do that", said Joe, "and you should have known that about me by now", he continued.
"Personally I think we should continue this conversation somewhere else", said Joe, trying to end this embarrassment for his friend.
"No, this conversation is over, and I'm 'outta here",

Craig said angrily. Craig headed back to his house, muttering under his breath about Joe being some friend, and why these things always happened to him. He just couldn't seem to understand that he brought these things on himself with his lies.

When Craig arrived home, he was surprised to see his Dad's car in the driveway, meaning he was back early from his business trip. He ran into the house glad his Dad was back and wanted to see him. "Hi

Dad, glad you're home", said Craig to his dad.
"Hello son, I'm glad to be home also, that is until I found out some things", his dad said slowly. "Why have you lied to your mother about having your jobs done when they haven't even been started", his father asked sternly.

Craig hung his head knowing he was no longer going to fool his dad. "I don't know, I was late for the game and didn't want to miss it", he said.
"Craig, I'm really getting tired of all of these lies you keep telling. You didn't do this when you did, or did do that when you didn't", his father sternly said.
"We are going to put a stop to this now", his dad

continued, "I hope you aren't doing this with your friends also. They will soon want nothing to do with you if you are, at least the ones worth having as friends", he said.

Craig thought of his friend Joe, and how he is always honest and truthful. He knows everyone loves that about him, and even if they do make fun of him sometimes for it, he always stands his ground. "I'm sorry Dad", Craig said. "Well I hope you really are, but sorry won't do it. For the next month you are to come home directly after school and do any chores your mom or I have for you. You can then have some time for yourself, at home of course, before you begin your homework. Weekends you will do extra things around the house. After two weekends, if everything has been done correctly with no lies, we'll see about the following weekends", his Dad said. "And Craig, the next lie I catch you in will double this punishment, so be very careful what you tell us", his dad finished. "OK Dad, I'll get this corrected", Craig said, with a new resolve to do it.

At school the next day Craig approached Joe and said, "Joe I'm really sorry for all of my lying, and especially trying to bring you into it with the guys the other day". Joe looked at his friend and said, "Craig,

the fact you are admitting it goes a long way with me. "Yeah, well my Dad got home early and caught me in the lies to my mother. I will have jobs to do every night after school and grounded from weekends for a couple of weeks, but I'm glad it happened; I know things were getting out of control", Craig said.
"It'll all be worth it", said Joe, "Trust me".

After school the boys headed home together, and Craig was feeling much better for putting the lying behind him.

MORAL OF THE STORY

Craig, like so many others, get caught up in lying to cover themselves for what they have done, or what they have not done. He could see the respect Joe always had because he was always honest, and people knew they could trust him.

Being truthful is one of the most important traits a person can have, because people notice it, and the integrity of the honest person makes it much easier to get ahead in life.

ABOUT THE AUTHOR

Richard L. McBain is the father of two adult sons, and a husband of forty-seven years. He worked as a youth counselor for teenage wards of a county in Ohio, and later as a director of three corporations. He has held the positions of Chief Operating Officer, General Manager, and/or Vice President of six different companies. He now serves as President and CEO Triune Group, Inc. in Marietta, Georgia.

Dick McBain, 70, has been a Christian all of his life and a student of the Bible for the last 41 years. He has authored and published three other books and wanted to help children learn about morals and manners in a fun way through short stories that would interest them. He has four grand-children and believes the kids today need some help learning these important principles.

Made in the USA
Las Vegas, NV
07 March 2021